Naughty Fairies

Imps are Wimps!

Collect all the Naughty Fairies books:

Imps are Wimps!

Lucy Mayflower

Hodder
Children's
Books

A division of Hachette Children's Books

Special thanks to Lucy Courtenay

Created by Hodder Children's Books and Lucy Courtenay
Text and illustrations copyright © 2006 Hodder Children's Books
Illustrations created by Artful Doodlers

First published in Great Britain in 2006
by Hodder Children's Books

4

A Catalogue record for this book is available from the British Library

ISBN-10: 0 340 91177 8
ISBN-13: 9780340911778

Printed and bound in Great Britain
by Bookmarque Ltd, Croydon, Surrey

The paper and board used in this paperback by Hodder Children's Books
are natural recyclable products made from wood grown in
sustainable forests. The manufacturing processes conform to the
environmental regulations of the country of origin.

Hodder Children's Books
A division of Hachette Children's Books
338 Euston Rd, London NW1 3BH

Contents

Ambrosia Academy

WOOD STUMP

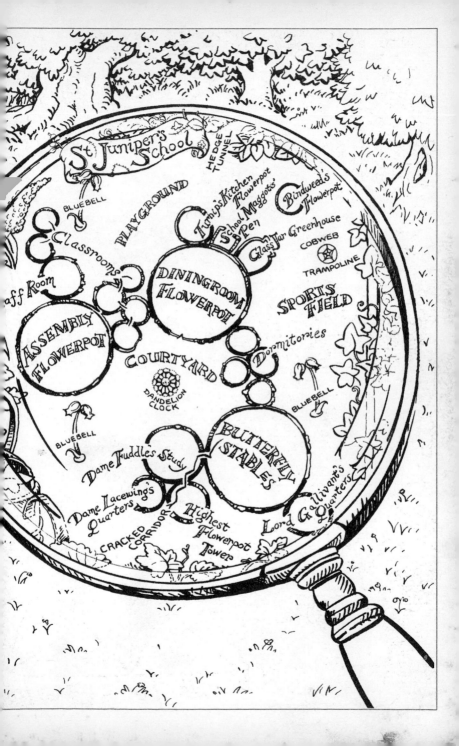

1

Fairy Dust

Down at the bottom of the garden, there is a pile of flowerpots behind an old watering can and a patch of nettles. A dandelion clock grows in the middle, and bluebells grow around the edges. The flowerpots aren't much to look at. This is probably why you never noticed them before.

Look more closely. You will see an extraordinary thing. The flowerpots have tiny doors and windows. This is St Juniper's, the famous fairy school. It is famous for many reasons, mostly bad ones. Don't worry if you've never heard of it. You're not a fairy, after all.

The flowerpot nearest the Hedge is

the Fairy Science classroom. For the next forty dandelion seeds, the fairies are going to have a Fairy Science lesson. To fairies, dandelion seeds are like minutes, and whole dandelions are like hours.

Take a peep at the fairies sitting near the back. There are five of them, and their names are Brilliance, Nettle, Sesame, Kelpie and Tiptoe. They are the naughtiest fairies in the whole of St Juniper's, and that's saying something.

Shh! Can you hear the bluebells ringing? The St Juniper's dandelion clock is about to lose its first seed. It's time for Fairy Science to begin.

Brilliance was bored. She stretched her wings and flapped them. Petal pages fluttered off the fairies' desks and floated to the floor.

"Who is flapping?" Dame Taffeta asked the class.

Dame Taffeta was the Fairy Science teacher. The most interesting thing about Dame Taffeta was her ears. When she got annoyed, they turned pink. Last week, her ears had turned red. It had been the best Fairy Science lesson ever.

Brilliance sat very still.

Dame Taffeta turned back to the large grey rock beside her. She tapped her fairy wand on the rockboard. A piece of chalk appeared on the tip of the wand. Dame Taffeta squiggled some chalk on the rockboard. "By separating the *stalk* from the *leaf*," Dame Taffeta said, "you . . ."

Brilliance flapped her wings a little harder. She rose very slightly off her seat. By the time Dame Taffeta turned round, Brilliance was sitting down again. She gave Dame Taffeta one of her brilliant smiles.

Dame Taffeta's ears began to change colour.

"Stop it, Brilliance," Nettle whispered. "Dame Taffeta always gives us tests when her ears turn pink."

Nettle was Brilliance's best friend. She had short blonde hair. Two tiny spiders dangled from Nettle's ears, and she had mud on her chin.

"I don't want to make stupid baby lullaby spells," Brilliance said. "I don't want to make fluffy bunny dream spells. I want to know how to turn Dame Taffeta's nose blue. I want to know how to grow a honeycake tree. *Useful* stuff."

"Have a dew chew," Nettle said. She offered Brilliance a glittery sweet.

The dew chew gave Brilliance an idea.

"You're smiling," Nettle said with interest. "What are you planning?"

Brilliance smiled wider. "Have you got any more dew chews?" she asked.

Nettle put two more on the desk.

Brilliance was disappointed. "Is that all you've got?"

Nettle shrugged. "I ate the rest," she said. "Ask the others."

Brilliance kicked the small, dark-haired fairy sitting on her other side. "Tiptoe?" she said. "Have you got any dew chews?"

"Yes," Tiptoe said cautiously. Tiptoe always had food. "But I was saving them."

"Saving them for what?" Brilliance demanded.

"For when I get hungry," Tiptoe said.

"I'll swap them for tonight's pudding," Brilliance offered. "It's raspberry cream."

Dame Taffeta stared at them rather hard. Brilliance gave another brilliant smile. Nettle and Tiptoe sat up very straight in their chairs.

"Pay attention at the back," Dame Taffeta said. Her ears looked a little pinker.

"Yes, Dame Taffeta."

Dame Taffeta turned back to her chalk squiggles.

Tiptoe pulled a honeycake, a beech-nut sandwich and seven dew chews out of her pocket. She passed the dew chews to Brilliance and ate the beech-nut sandwich. Then, as she reached for the honeycake, a large bumblebee zoomed through the flowerpot and snatched it up.

"Kelpie!" Tiptoe complained to the red-haired fairy sitting in front of her.

"Can't you control your bumblebee?"

Kelpie shrugged.

"Flea's hungry," she said.

"Have you got any dew chews, Kelpie?" Brilliance asked, leaning across her desk.

"No," Kelpie said.

"Flea doesn't like dew chews," Brilliance coaxed. "They make his teeth stick together."

"Flea doesn't have teeth, stupid," Kelpie said.

"Sesame?" Brilliance asked the fairy sitting on the other side of Kelpie.

Sesame gave a dew chew to Brilliance. Then she went back to stroking her pet caterpillar, Sprout, who was lying on her lap. Sprout was large and green. Right now, he was snoring.

Brilliance warmed all the dew chews

in her hands. She rolled
them together into a sticky
ball. Then she threw the
ball as hard as she could.
It flew into the air and
stuck high up on the
flowerpot ceiling.

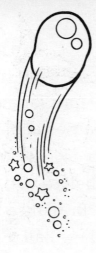

Brilliant, she thought
with satisfaction.

Dame Taffeta's voice suddenly floated
into Brilliance's ears.

" . . . five dandelion seeds to make the fairy dust. If you have been listening," Dame Taffeta glanced at the Naughty Fairies again, "then you will know what to do. The ingredients are on the shelves. Off you go."

Brilliance looked away from the dew chew ball. She stared at her four friends, who all stared back. Nobody had heard Dame Taffeta's instructions about making fairy dust.

"OK," Brilliance said. "It can't be hard. Let's try this . . . and this . . . and this." She grabbed three small acorn cups of leaves, seeds and beetle wings from the nearest shelf, and put them on the table.

Tiptoe put her nose to the nearest pot and sniffed. "Pooh," she said. "Fairy dust doesn't smell like that."

"Got any better ideas?" Brilliance demanded.

There were two walnut shells beside

the flowerpot door. One was full of rainwater, and the other was full of dew.

"Nettle, go and get some rainwater," Brilliance said.

"Don't you mean dew?" Nettle asked. Nettle was better at Fairy Science than Brilliance.

"It doesn't matter," Brilliance said impatiently.

Sesame picked up Sprout and put him on the floor. She gave him a piece of grass to chew on. "I think it probably does matter, Brilliance," she began.

"Whatever," Brilliance sighed. She looked out of the window at the St Juniper's dandelion clock. Two dandelion seeds fell off and floated away on the wind. "We've only got three dandelion seeds left," she said. "Hurry up!"

Nettle collected some rainwater. Brilliance gave a big leaf, a small leaf, and a medium-sized seed to Kelpie.

"Mash these, will you, Kelpie?"
Brilliance asked.

"No," Kelpie said.

Brilliance gave Kelpie one of her
brilliant smiles. Kelpie took the leaves
and the seed.

"Tiptoe, fetch an acorn cup from
Dame Taffeta's desk," Brilliance
ordered. "Sesame, we need a pebble
from the pebble box on the window sill.
Now – quick!"

Tiptoe and Sesame fetched the acorn
cup and the pebble. Kelpie put the
leaves and the seed in the acorn cup.
Then she bashed them hard with the
pebble. Soon they turned into mush.
Nettle added a drop of rainwater, and
Brilliance stirred the mixture. Sesame
added some blue beetle wings.

They all stared into the cup.

"It doesn't look like dust," said Tiptoe.

Brilliance rolled her eyes. "It's still
wet," she said. "We have to boil it

before it turns into dust."

The five fairies carried the acorn cup to the nearest firefly. The firefly was cold and quiet. Sesame tickled the firefly under the chin, until it wriggled and started to glow. Brilliance put the acorn cup on the firefly and stirred it until the mixture started bubbling.

"Is it supposed to be that colour?" Sesame asked.

"It's brilliant," said Brilliance with determination. Her friends looked a bit doubtful.

"One dandelion seed!" Dame Taffeta announced to the class.

Nettle looked at the chalk squiggles on the rockboard. "We're supposed to say some magic words," she said. "Dame Taffeta has written something on the rock. Try that."

Brilliance picked up her wand and waved it around. She read the words on the rockboard. *"Humulus lupulus!"*

There was a loud bang as the acorn cup exploded. Beetle wings and bubbling gunge splattered the walls. Sprout squeaked and tried to hide between Sesame's feet.

"Twinkle-tastic," Kelpie said admiringly.

Dame Taffeta's ears had turned dark purple. She opened her mouth. "What . . . you . . . urgh!" she said.

"Uh-oh," Brilliance said, staring at the ceiling.

The dew chew ball had dropped with

a squelch on Dame Taffeta's head.

"Test!" Dame Taffeta shrieked.

2

Crawly Catching

That evening, Brilliance and her four
friends sat on St Juniper's highest
flowerpot tower. Flea the bumblebee
zigzagged through the air above them.

They could see everything from up
here.

In the Sports Field, Bindweed the
garden pixie was tying his team of ants
to a twig, ready to cut the grass.

By the Butterfly Stables, Lord
Gallivant the butterfly-riding teacher
was grooming Plankton, his Red
Admiral butterfly.

Down in the courtyard, Dame Fuddle,
Head Fairy of St Juniper's, was
teaching Fairy Deportment. Ten fairies

were walking around the courtyard in a circle, trying to balance apple pips on their heads.

"Who cares if fairies stand up straight?" Kelpie said, staring down at the Fairy Deportment class. "You can't stand up straight when you're flying."

"I have a brilliant plan," Brilliance announced. "To get us out of Dame

Taffeta's fairy dust test tomorrow. Naughty Fairies!"

She stuck out her fist.

No one said anything.

"Doesn't anyone want to hear my plan?" Brilliance demanded, dropping her fist.

"No," Kelpie said. She threw a honeycake in the air for Flea to catch.

"But you'll tell us anyway," Nettle said, flitting into a sparkling somersault and landing on the other side of the flowerpot tower.

"I'm trying to get us out of trouble," Brilliance said patiently.

"*You're* the one in trouble," Tiptoe said. "Dame Taffeta knows you made the dew chew ball."

Brilliance glared at her. "We've all got to take the fairy dust test, haven't we?" she said. She stuck out her fist again. "Naughty Fairies!"

"Do we have to do this NF thing

every time one of us has a plan?" Sesame moaned. "I can never think of anything."

"That's because you can't spell," said Kelpie, putting her fist on Brilliance's. "Niggle flaptart."

"Flaptart's not a word," Nettle said.

"Well, it should be," said Kelpie. "Come on Nettle. Your turn, or we'll be here all night."

"Nicely framed," said Nettle, and put her fist on Kelpie's.

Tiptoe whistled. "Good one," she said. "Um . . . nimble fingers?"

"Knicker fart!" Sesame giggled, and put her fist on Tiptoe's.

"Knicker starts with a 'k'," said Brilliance.

Sesame looked astonished. "Does it?"

Brilliance shook her head impatiently. "Never mind. Fly, fly . . . "

" . . . to the SKY!" the others chanted, and lifted their hands into the air.

"So," Brilliance said, "here's the plan. Let's go into the meadow and capture some crawlies tonight."

"Twinkle-tastic," Sesame said happily, tickling Sprout. She loved crawlies.

"When we have enough crawlies, we'll bring them back to school," Brilliance said. "We'll hide them near the Science Flowerpot for the night. Then, when Dame Taffeta gives out the test tomorrow, we'll let the crawlies into the flowerpot. We'll spend the whole lesson chasing the crawlies out again and no one will have time for the test. Isn't it a brilliant plan?"

"How do we get the crawlies inside?" Nettle asked.

"We tie them to a piece of spider silk," Brilliance said. "I'll tug the silk, and they'll come through the window."

"Wow," Sesame breathed. "All those crawlies."

"We must make sure we're back in time for dinner," Tiptoe said. "It's already five past the dandelion, and dinner's at five to."

Brilliance looked down at the courtyard. Dame Fuddle had gone, and the Fairy Deportment class were now throwing their apple pips at each other and yelling. "Let's go before Dame

21

Fuddle comes back!" she said. She flexed her wings and jumped off the flowerpot tower.

Nettle jumped off next. Then Tiptoe. Sesame tucked Sprout down the front of her dress, and had to beat her wings extra hard to stay in the air. Kelpie hopped on Flea's back and dug her knees into his furry sides so that he zoomed after the others.

They headed for the Hedge Tunnel in a straggly line. Everything went cool and dark as they raced through the Tunnel. Then everything burst into light again as they shot out the other side. They were on the edge of the Meadow.

The Meadow was huge. Tall green grasses waved overhead. There were red poppies and pink campion. There were white daisies and blue forget-me-nots. And most importantly, there were lots and lots of crawlies.

Brilliance landed on a hairy primrose

leaf, and straightened her skirt.

Sesame landed next to Brilliance. "Sprout, you weigh as much as a walnut," she complained, as Sprout wriggled out of her dress with a nervous squeak. "When you're a butterfly, you can carry me."

Flea was puffing loudly. He landed on the primrose leaf with a flump. His wings lay crumpled at his side, and he looked a bit tired. Kelpie hopped off his back and fed him a honeycake.

Tiptoe landed, and then fell over. This was normal. "Why do you always ride Flea, Kelpie?" Tiptoe asked, dusting off her knees as she stood up.

"I hate my wings," Kelpie said. "They're stupid and glittery. Anyway, Flea needs to get fit."

Nettle was the last one to land. There was no sign of her ear spiders. After a moment, they peeped out nervously. Then they spun their silk, and dangled

24

from Nettle's ears again.

"We need to make lassos to catch the crawlies," Brilliance said. "Will your spiders let us have some silk, Nettle?"

Nettle took the tiny spiders from her ears. She put them on the edge of a yellow primrose petal, where they started spinning silk happily.

Soon, the fairies had five strong lassos. Tiptoe whirled hers over her head and lassoed Sesame. Kelpie tested hers on Flea. Nettle flung her lasso over a nearby flower. She hung upside down and swung there for a bit.

"Aren't you going to test your lasso, Brilliance?" Nettle asked.

"What for?" said Brilliance. "It's bound to be brilliant."

The five fairies agreed to meet back on the primrose leaf in ten dandelion seeds. Brilliance whirred her wings and headed into a damp patch of grass. She tried her lasso on a woodlouse, but the

woodlouse rolled into a ball and the
lasso fell off. Then she tried a worm, but
it slithered away before she tightened
the loop. Crawly catching was harder
than it looked.

Suddenly a very long millipede
waddled out of the grass towards
Brilliance. It was fat and coppery

brown, and it waved its antennae at her.
Brilliance twirled her lasso in the air
and flung it neatly over the millipede's
head.

Very slowly, Brilliance started pulling.

The millipede dug five hundred of its
feet into the ground.

Brilliance pulled again.

The millipede dug in its other five hundred feet.

Brilliance felt herself slowly being pulled forward.

This wasn't going to plan.

Then something caught Brilliance's attention through the grass stalks behind the millipede. A small blue imp was scuttling through the meadow. On his back was a large box, and the box was stamped with the words:

PERFECT FAIRY DUST
INGREDIENTS.
GUARANTEED 100%
SATISFACTION.

Brilliance almost let go of the millipede. Ingredients for the test!

"Hey!" she called in excitement. "Hey! Over here!"

The imp scuttled faster. He didn't look at Brilliance.

PERFECT
FAIRY DUST
INGREDIENTS
GUARANTEED
100%
SATISFACTION

Brilliance suddenly remembered something about imps. Three things, actually.

Imps never gave you anything you asked for.

They hated insults.

And they loved millipedes.

"Hey, sheep tick!" Brilliance shouted.

"Your ugly face could crack a nut!"

The imp stopped. He peered through the grass.

"You're stupider than a twig!" Brilliance shouted again. "Your breath smells of bat wee!"

The imp came charging through the grass towards her. "You fairy fruitcake!" he yelled. "You . . . you . . . that's a nice millipede." His voice changed from

angry to interested.

"I know," Brilliance said. She hung on to the millipede with all her strength. The millipede reared up and waved a hundred legs in the air. "I'm just taking it for a walk."

"I've always wanted a millipede," the imp said.

"So?" Brilliance said. "This one's not for sale."

The imp flared his blue nostrils at her. "I'll swap you," he said.

Brilliance tried not to look at the box of fairy dust ingredients on the imp's back. "It's not for sale," she repeated.

The imp looked cunning. "I'll swap you these fairy dust ingredients for the millipede," he said. He reached out a thin blue hand and stroked the millipede's head.

"Why would I want your smelly fairy dust ingredients?" Brilliance said.

"They work every time," the imp

grinned. "You can make perfect fairy dust, ten times over."

Brilliance sighed, like she'd just made a very difficult decision. "OK," she said reluctantly. "I suppose you can have my millipede. Goodbye . . . Wiggle."

"Hello, Wiggle," the imp said happily, stroking the millipede under the chin. He put down his box of ingredients and

hopped on to the millipede's back. The millipede tried to bite him. The imp looked delighted.

Brilliance snatched up the box of fairy dust ingredients and flew back to the primrose leaf.

The other fairies were waiting for her.

Kelpie had four ants. She was tying them to Flea's tummy with spider silk.

Sesame had a beetle and a wasp on two grass leads. Sprout was sniffing the beetle's bottom.

Nettle and Tiptoe were sitting on the back of a large green cricket.

"What's in the box?" Kelpie asked Brilliance.

"I'll tell you back at school," Brilliance said.

Kelpie jumped on Flea, who rose unsteadily into the air. The ants waved their feet around feebly.

Sesame put Sprout inside her dress. She tightened her grip on the wasp and

the beetle. Then she clicked her tongue. The two creatures zoomed upwards so fast that Sesame was soon out of sight.

Nettle and Tiptoe dug their heels into the cricket's sides. The cricket jumped towards the hedge.

Brilliance flew close behind Flea and Kelpie. She stared happily at her box of perfect fairy dust ingredients.

"Brilliant," she said.

3

Magic Seeds

The fairies peeped into the school
courtyard. The dandelion clock still had
a quarter of its seeds.

"Phew," Tiptoe said, from high up on
the cricket's back. "We haven't missed
dinner."

Sesame's beetle tried to bite one of
the ants tied to Flea's tummy.

"We've got to take the crawlies to the
Science Flowerpot and give them
something to eat," Sesame said. At the
mention of eating, Sprout stuck his
head out of the top of her dress
and squeaked.

"You still haven't told us what's in
your box, Brilliance," Nettle said.

"Perfect fairy dust ingredients," Brilliance said. "I swapped them for a millipede."

Sesame looked disappointed. "Don't we need the crawlies any more?"

"The crawlies are now Plan B," Brilliance said. "In case these ingredients don't work. Take the crawlies to the Science Flowerpot, like we planned. I'm going to the dormitory to look inside my box."

Brilliance shared a dormitory with the others in one of the smaller flowerpots. There were five leaf beds, lined with feathers. There was a foxglove sleeping bag and a wool pillow on each bed. A long tin-foil mirror was stuck to one wall. By the door there was a walnut shell full of rainwater for washing.

Brilliance went to her bed, and put the box down. She opened the lid. Inside the box were three black seeds, which Brilliance put on the bed. Then

she turned the box upside down and shook it.

There were no instructions.

"Who needs instructions?" Brilliance said to herself. "They're just seeds."

She flew out of the window and filled the empty box with soil. Then she put the box down by the dormitory window

and pushed the seeds into the damp
earth. She fetched a handful of
rainwater from the walnut shell, and
sprinkled it on top.

Outside, a bluebell started ringing.
The dandelion clock was down to its
last five seeds, which meant it was time
for dinner.

Brilliance flew out of the window and
zoomed towards the Dining Flowerpot.
Clusters of fairies were giggling and
pushing through the flowerpot door.
Their wings made a strong breeze,
which blew the remaining seeds off the
dandelion clock.

Inside the flowerpot, her friends were
waiting.

"So?" Nettle asked, as they reached
the food counter. "What were these
ingredients like?"

"They were seeds," Brilliance said.
She helped herself to sorrel salad and
poppy bread. "I planted them. Hope

they hurry up and grow."

"Bet they don't," Kelpie snorted. She put six honeycakes on her plate.

"How are the crawlies?" Brilliance asked Sesame.

"The beetle ate one of the ants," Sesame said. "But the others are all fine."

The St Juniper's staff members were at a long bark table at the end of the Dining Flowerpot. Dame Fuddle sat in

the middle. Next to her was Dame
Lacewing, her Deputy. Dame Lacewing
taught Fairy Maths. Lord Gallivant was
arguing with Bindweed the garden
pixie at one end of the table. Dame
Taffeta giggled with the Fairy English
teacher, Dame Honey, at the other end.
Legless the school earthworm was lying
on the floor in front of the table. He
stretched the whole way from Lord
Gallivant to Dame Honey.

The five Naughty Fairies found an empty bark table near the door and sat down.

"What if the seeds don't grow?" Tiptoe asked.

"Then we turn to Plan B, stupid," Kelpie said. "The crawlies."

"What are the seeds going to grow into?" Nettle asked.

Brilliance poured herself a glass of elderflower juice. "Don't ask me," she said.

The fairies had a dandelion of free time before bed. Brilliance and the others went to the Butterfly Stables to do some butterfly riding. They were late because Tiptoe had gone back for seconds.

Butterfly riding was very popular at St Juniper's, and the Butterfly Stables were in the school's largest flowerpot. The flowerpot was divided into four sections: eggs, caterpillars, pupae and butterflies. In the butterfly section, three tatty Cabbage Whites sat snoozing in their stalls. The largest one's wings were so ragged that it didn't look like it would be able to fly at all.

"There're only three left," Brilliance said, staring inside the stalls. "The rest must be out flying already."

"And they're rubbish ones too," Kelpie said. "This is your fault, Tiptoe."

Tiptoe blushed. There was a bit of raspberry cream on her chin.

Lord Gallivant came into the stables. He bowed at the fairies, tossed his blond hair and stroked one of his pointed ears. Lord Gallivant was an Elf. He was also a former Midsummer Champion Butterfly Racer. It was difficult not to know this, because he talked about it all the time.

"There are just two butterflies available tonight, little fairies," he trilled. "Snowball has a cold, and can't go out. Of course, when I won the Midsummer Champion Butterfly Race, my butterfly had pneumonia. But the talent lies with the rider." He smiled modestly.

The largest Cabbage White sneezed. A bit of powder fell off his wings.

"Poor Snowball," Sesame said.

"I don't care," Kelpie said. "I hate riding butterflies anyway. I'll ride Flea."

"I shall ride Salt," Brilliance said, marching over to the least ragged of the three Cabbage Whites.

There was only one butterfly left. Nettle stared hard at the raspberry cream on Tiptoe's chin.

"I don't want to ride a butterfly tonight," Tiptoe said reluctantly.

"Good," Nettle said. "Sesame?"

"I'll groom Snowball," Sesame said. She picked up a pot of butterfly powder sitting by the stable door.

Nettle smiled. "I'll take Chalky then," she said. "Race you to the watering can, Brilliance!"

Brilliance and Nettle swooped out of the Butterfly Stables side by side. There was a swirl of butterfly powder in the air as they raced into the pale pink evening sky.

Brilliance won the race.

"I won because I'm brilliant," Brilliance boasted, powdering Salt's wings.

"You won because you cheated," Nettle said moodily, giving Chalky some nectar.

The sun had almost set and the garden was dark. Brilliance and Nettle said goodbye to the butterflies and flew up to their dormitory window. Climbing carefully over Flea, who was curled up in a furry ball on the window sill, Brilliance and Nettle flopped into their leaf beds.

"Today was a good day," Brilliance said. She thought of the dew chew ball,

and the crawlies, and her magic seeds, and she smiled.

"Pretty good," Nettle agreed sleepily. She put her two little ear spiders on her acorn bedside table.

Tiptoe gave a gentle snore. Sprout, lying at the end of Sesame's bed, gave a slightly louder one.

"Night, everyone," Sesame said with a yawn.

"I hate bedtime," Kelpie grumbled. "I'd much rather . . . mmm . . ."

The magic seeds started to tremble in their earth bed. But the fairies didn't notice. They were all fast asleep.

4

The Big Stink

Something was tickling Brilliance's
nose. She opened her eyes. A leaf hung
over her bed like a green curtain.

"Wake up, everyone!" Brilliance
shouted. "The seeds are growing!"

The other fairies woke up. Sprout
squeaked and dived inside Sesame's
foxglove sleeping bag.

"Ooh!" Sesame gasped. This might
have been because Sprout was cold.

"It's huge!" Nettle yelled.

"It's incredible!" Tiptoe squealed.

"It's green!" Kelpie said sarcastically.
"Big wow."

The plant pushed underneath
Brilliance's bed, and tipped Brilliance

on to the floor. "We have to get out of here," Brilliance said. "Now!"

The fairies all scrambled out of bed.

"Flea!" Kelpie called. "Where are you?"

Flea buzzed crossly from outside. A large leaf had pushed him out of the window. He zoomed into the morning sky as the fairies ran towards their dormitory door.

"What about Flea?" Kelpie demanded, running after her friends.

"He can look after himself!" Brilliance shouted back.

Tendrils were shooting up through the hole in the flowerpot roof. The plant's fat green stem was whooshing down the corridor like a fat green snake. Leaves were everywhere.

Dame Lacewing appeared at the end of the corridor. She was wearing a cobweb nightgown and a very fierce expression. "What is this?" Dame Lacewing demanded, staring up at the huge plant.

"It's a plant, Dame Lacewing," Tiptoe answered.

"I can see that," Dame Lacewing said. She stamped on a tendril which was trying to climb up her leg. "But why is it so large? And what is it?"

Brilliance stayed very quiet. So did the others. Dame Lacewing stared hard at them. "We must evacuate the dormitories immediately," she said. "Go

to the Dining Flowerpot at once."

The Naughty Fairies climbed through the snaking plant towards the Dining Flowerpot. The plant was still growing, so gaps were there one minute and gone the next. It got harder and harder to push their way through. Other fairies joined them, pushing and shoving and shouting and squealing.

"What are we going to do?" Nettle hissed, when they reached the Dining Flowerpot.

"No one saw me plant the seeds," Brilliance said.

"They're in our dormitory," Sesame said, cuddling Sprout.

"They're next to your bed," Tiptoe added.

"You are *so* in trouble," Kelpie grinned.

Brilliance tossed her hair. "I don't care," she said.

Fairies from all over St Juniper's were

streaming into the Dining Flowerpot.
The plant was now beginning to climb
through the windows there. Tendrils
were cascading down the walls and
bursting into leaf.

"I hope Flea's OK," said Kelpie
anxiously, peering out of the windows.

"He'll be fine," Sesame assured her.

All the St Juniper's members of staff
stood at the long bark table.

Bindweed the garden pixie had his
team of leaf-cutting ants on six grass
leashes. The ants were staring hungrily
at a nearby tendril.

Lord Gallivant had forgotten to take a
curler out of his hair.

Turnip the kitchen pixie was wearing
a rose-petal apron and a furious
expression. But this was normal.

Dame Honey, Dame Taffeta and
Dame Lacewing were talking to Dame
Fuddle in low voices and they were all
looking worried.

At last, Dame Fuddle turned towards
the St Juniper's pupils. She waved her
wand for attention, and sparks shot into
the air. The fairies fell quiet.

"My dear fairies!" Dame Fuddle said.
"Disaster!" Dame Fuddle often spoke in
exclamation marks. "The staff and I
must find this plant's roots and stop it
growing! All fairies must stay in the

Dining Flowerpot! Lessons are cancelled until further notice!"

The fairies cheered. It was Fairy Maths that morning. Chattering happily, they all made their way to the food counters for breakfast. But the food counters were bare.

"No breakfast," Turnip the kitchen pixie growled. "That plant has taken over my kitchen."

"No breakfast?" Tiptoe said in dismay.

Turnip folded his arms. "None," he said. "Unless ye fetch it yeself."

"We're not allowed out of the Dining Flowerpot," Sesame said.

"Then ye'll have to stay hungry," Turnip said.

The hungry fairies went and sat down.

"Dame Fuddle was right," Tiptoe said sadly. "This is a disaster."

"I don't care," Kelpie growled. "I hate breakfast."

"They've probably found the plant roots in our dormitory by now," Nettle said. "What are we going to say?"

"They can't prove we did it," Brilliance said.

"*You* did it," Sesame said. "Not us."

"Brilliant!" Brilliance suddenly gasped, and put her fist on the table. "I've just thought of something. Naughty Fairies!"

The fairies waited for what felt like ten dandelions. At last, Dame Fuddle and Dame Lacewing came back to the Dining Flowerpot.

"Would Brilliance, Nettle, Sesame, Tiptoe and Kelpie please stand up!" Dame Fuddle said.

The five fairies stood up. All the other fairies stared at them.

"It would seem this plant is growing in a box by your dormitory window!" Dame Fuddle said.

"That's terrible, Dame Fuddle," Brilliance said. "That makes it look like we planted it."

Dame Fuddle frowned. "Are you saying that you *didn't* plant it?"

"I think it was a bird, Dame Fuddle," Nettle said.

"How can a bird plant a seed?" Dame Fuddle asked.

The Naughty Fairies looked at each other.

"By pooing," Kelpie said.

There was a shocked silence. All the fairies in the room started giggling.

"I beg your pardon?" Dame Fuddle said at last.

"You know," Kelpie said. "Pooing. Birds poo seeds all the time."

Dame Fuddle looked a bit faint. The fairies giggled louder.

"Through a window?" Dame Lacewing asked. "Into a box?"

Brilliance gave one of her most brilliant smiles. "It's possible, Dame Lacewing," she said. "Isn't it?"

All the fairies started chattering. Dame Fuddle waved her wand for silence again. "This is not the end of the matter!" she said. "Dame Honey and Dame Taffeta are still working on the problem! If the plant continues to grow, we shall have to evacuate the entire school!"

"What about the ants?" one of the fairies called out.

"Bindweed has tried his ants," Dame Lacewing said. "They have done their best, but they have eaten the leaves in only half the dormitories. Now they're tired, and are sleeping."

"I'll need the ants in my kitchen next," Turnip said loudly. "Or there'll be no food for the rest of the day."

"Bindweed says that the ants will sleep for at least two dandelions!" Dame Fuddle said, wringing her hands. "By the time they wake up, the plant will have replaced all its leaves! We shall have to start again!"

Brilliance put her hand in the air. "Dame Fuddle?" she said. "I think the plant has stopped growing."

All the fairies stopped chattering. They stared around at the plant. For the first time, it looked still and silent. The fairies cheered, and Nettle did three sparkling somersaults in a row. Even Turnip smiled, a bit.

"What a relief!" Dame Fuddle said, and fanned herself with her wand. Sprinkles of light fell through the air.

Dame Lacewing said nothing. She tapped her fingers on the long bark table, and stared very hard at Brilliance. Brilliance stared back, and didn't blink once.

*

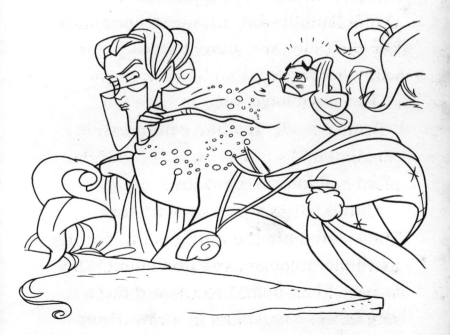

When the ants woke up, Bindweed brought them straight to the kitchen to clear it. Then Turnip was able to cook a late breakfast while the ants went back to work on the dormitories. Soon, the Dining Flowerpot was filled with the smell of hot seed bread and roasted pine nuts.

"This isn't so bad," Tiptoe said. "We aren't in trouble, we don't have Fairy Maths, and this bread is delicious."

"I wish Flea was here, though," Kelpie said gloomily.

"The plant looks nice in here too," Brilliance said. "It's like eating inside the Hedge."

They all looked up at the ceiling.

"I think it's growing again," said Nettle suddenly.

The plant had started producing large flowers. They hung high above all the fairy tables like yellow bells and looked very pretty.

The first flower opened. The scent
wafted down to the Naughty Fairies'
table.

"Urgh!" Brilliance gagged.

"Euw!" Nettle choked.

"Bleugh!" Sesame wept. Sprout's eyes
began to water.

"Ick, ick, ick!" Tiptoe flapped her
arms around.

"That is totally disgusting," Kelpie
said happily.

5

Imps are Wimps!

More yellow bellflowers opened their petals. The Dining Flowerpot filled with an awful stink. Lord Gallivant burst into tears and flew out of the nearest window. Dame Fuddle seized her petal napkin and pressed it to her face.

Dame Lacewing waved her wand above her head. *"Rosa canina!"*

The smell of summer roses washed through the air. For a few moments, the fairies could breathe again.

"Evacuate!" Dame Fuddle shouted, lifting her nose from her petal napkin.

"The yellow flowers have almost blocked the door!" Sesame said.

"And the windows!" Tiptoe added.

"How are we going to get out of here?" Nettle asked.

"Who wants to get out?" Kelpie said. She reached for a yellow flower and sniffed it. "It's cool in here."

Because of the flowers, the door to the courtyard was now completely blocked. Every time a yellow bellflower opened, the smell got worse. The rose spell wasn't working any more.

Dame Lacewing waved her wand again. *"Viola odorata!"*

Now the fairies could smell violets. But the problem was getting worse. The Dining Flowerpot was growing dark as the flowers cut out all the light.

"We'll have to go through the dormitories," Brilliance guessed. "The ants have eaten half the plant in there. Maybe we can get outside that way."

"Through the dormitories!" Dame Lacewing called, as if she'd heard Brilliance. "To the Butterfly Stables!"

All the fairies in the Dining Flowerpot rushed towards the dormitories. Thanks to the ants, the dormitory corridor was clear. The fairies shoved and screamed and shouted very unfairylike things at each other as they ran.

Butterflies fluttered in alarm as the fairies burst into the cool darkness of the Butterfly Stables.

"The plant's in here too!" Brilliance gasped, staring at the leaves snaking around the doors and windows. "There's no way out!"

"At least there are no yellow flowers," Nettle said.

"Yet," Kelpie added.

Brilliance parted some leaves and peered out of a window. She had a good view of the courtyard. Bindweed was gloomily squirting something at the yellow flowers. Lord Gallivant swooped into view on Plankton, his Red Admiral butterfly. "Keep it up, young pixie!" he called down to Bindweed. "Ignore the pong!"

Bindweed, who wasn't young, glared at him.

"When I won the Midsummer Champion Butterfly Race," Lord Gallivant continued, "the butterfly in front had terrible wind. But I didn't let it distract me! Oh no! I just pushed on and won!"

Bindweed turned his back on Lord Gallivant and gave the flowers an extra hard squirt.

"I can see Flea," Brilliance said suddenly.

Kelpie ran to her side. "Where is he?" she demanded. "Is he OK?"

Flea was buzzing around the flower-filled courtyard. He dived straight into a yellow flower with a stupid expression on his face.

"Urgh," Sesame shuddered, peering over Brilliance's shoulder. She cuddled

Sprout tightly. "How can Flea go anywhere near that flower?"

"He's a bee, stupid," Kelpie said. "That's what bees do."

Flea lurched out of the flower. He gave the bee equivalent of a burp.

"Flea looks bigger," Tiptoe said. "Don't you think?"

"Uh-oh," Brilliance said.

As they watched, Flea's body grew fatter. His wings stretched. His antennae lengthened. His buzz deepened to a kind of growl.

"That's amazing!" Kelpie shouted.

"He's growing as fast as the plant!"
Sesame squealed.

"It must be the nectar inside the
flowers!" Brilliance said.

Flea zoomed enthusiastically at
another yellow bell.

"We've just *got* to stop him!"
Nettle yelled.

Flea came out of the flower, burped again, and got even bigger.

There was a crack, and a spark. The fairies turned around.

"Your attention, fairies!" Dame Fuddle said, lowering her wand. She was hovering on her Orange Tip butterfly, Zest. "We can't stop these flowers growing, and outside we have a bumblebee the size of a hedgehog! The

Humans in the House will notice! This is the end for St Juniper's!"

Dame Lacewing was hovering next to Dame Fuddle, on her Meadow Brown butterfly, Fraction. "If anyone has any information," Dame Lacewing added, "please speak now. Before it is too late." She stared extremely hard at Brilliance.

Brilliance couldn't stop herself. She blinked.

Dame Lacewing flew across the flowerpot to where Brilliance and her friends were standing. She climbed off Fraction and stood in front of Brilliance.

"Brilliance," she said. Her voice was sharp. "Is there something you would like to say?"

"It was the imp's fault," Brilliance said. "He didn't give me any instructions."

"From the beginning please," Dame Lacewing said.

"I caught a millipede," Brilliance said

sulkily. "This imp wanted it. So I swapped him for the seeds. He didn't say not to plant them."

Dame Lacewing frowned. "What were these seeds for?"

"Fairy dust," Sesame said, stroking Sprout.

"Perfect fairy dust," Tiptoe added.

"We have a test this afternoon," Nettle said.

"Like I care," Kelpie muttered.

No one mentioned the crawlies they'd left by the Science Flowerpot.

"An imp, you say." Dame Lacewing folded her arms and drummed her fingertips on her elbows. "Do you know where this imp has gone?"

"I expect the millipede decided that," Brilliance said. "It was much bigger than the imp."

"We have no time to waste," Dame Lacewing said. "We must find this imp and get him to St Juniper's. What do you know about imps?"

"They never give you what you ask for," Brilliance said.

"They hate insults," answered Nettle.

"And they love millipedes," Sesame finished.

"Correct," Dame Lacewing said. "So we must attract this imp with an insult. And then make him fix the problem without asking him." She looked at Kelpie. "Any ideas?"

"Imps stink," Kelpie said.

"Not bad," Dame Lacewing nodded. "But I think we can do better. Anyone else?"

"Imps are thicker than pondweed!" suggested a pink-haired fairy at the back of the Butterfly Stables.

"Imps can't fart!" another fairy called.

"They can," Brilliance said. "They smell worse than these flowers."

"Really," Dame Fuddle said weakly, "must we talk of such things?"

"Imps are wimps!" Tiptoe announced.

"Aha!" Dame Lacewing swung around and pointed at Tiptoe. "Good!"

"How are we going to find the imp, Dame Lacewing?" Sesame asked.

"We're in here, and he's out there," Brilliance added.

"All in good time," Dame Lacewing said. "First, every fairy must take off one item of clothing."

Kelpie looked down at her black and yellow bumble-wool jumper dress. "I'm only wearing one item of clothing," she said.

"Then you'd better keep it on," Dame Lacewing said kindly. "Fetch some silk from the stable spider, Kelpie. We have some sewing to do."

All the other fairies took off one item of clothing. Soon there was a pile of clothes in the middle of the stable. Moss jumpers and nettle trousers. Feather tops, grass skirts and petal pants. Sweet-wrapper cardies. Dame Fuddle offered her favourite spider-silk scarf. Dame Lacewing took off her beautiful beech-leaf coat and added it to the pile. When all the clothes were laid out next to each other, they stretched the entire length of the Butterfly Stables.

The fairies sewed all the clothes together into a great multi-coloured banner. With everyone sewing, they finished the banner very quickly.

"And now for the finishing touch," Dame Lacewing said.

She raised her wand and twirled it three times. Light swooshed through the air. The light looped itself over and under and round, tying itself into the words: IMPS ARE WIMPS! Then the words floated down like feathers and settled on the banner.

"You still haven't explained what we are going to do, Dame Lacewing!" Dame Fuddle said. She stared sadly at her spider-silk scarf in the middle of the banner.

"We need some volunteers to take the banner to the highest flowerpot tower," Dame Lacewing said. "They must hang it out of a window and attract this imp's attention. Brilliance, Nettle, Kelpie, Tiptoe and Sesame?"

"We didn't volunteer, Dame Lacewing," Brilliance said.

"I'm volunteering you," Dame Lacewing said. "Unless you would prefer a detention?"

The Naughty Fairies shook their heads.

"Good," Dame Lacewing said.

A yellow bellflower began to bloom through a nearby window.

"This is our only hope," Dame Lacewing added, glancing anxiously at the flower. "Don't let us down!"

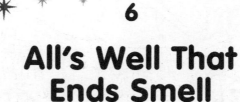

6

All's Well That Ends Smell

"Here goes," Brilliance said.

She picked up the front of the banner. Nettle picked up the back.

"It's heavy!" said Tiptoe.

"I can't see where I'm going!" Sesame complained. Sprout squeaked by her feet.

"It's not the imps who are wimps round here," Kelpie growled. She grabbed a middle section of the banner. "Let's use the Cracked Corridor."

Not many fairies knew about the Cracked Corridor. But Brilliance, Nettle, Sesame, Kelpie and Tiptoe used it all the time, to reach their favourite spot – the highest flowerpot tower.

The Cracked Corridor started halfway
up the Butterfly Stable wall. The fairies
scrambled over butterfly stalls and tried
not to tread on any wings as they
passed. When they reached the Cracked
Corridor, which led from the Butterfly
Stables to the top of Dame Fuddle's
study, they had to fold their wings very
tightly and then squeeze through
sideways. It was going to be nearly

impossible to pull the banner through as well.

The top of Dame Fuddle's study was usually open to the sky. Today, it had a thick green roof of leaves, tendrils and stinking yellow flowers, which hung down above them and swung gently in the wind. The fairies shuffled across, trying not to breathe through their noses.

"I'm going to be sick," Tiptoe said.

"Me too," Sesame said. Sprout squeaked and then sneezed.

"You lot are useless," Kelpie said scornfully.

"Stop squabbling," said Nettle.

"We're nearly at the Sideways Crack," Brilliance added. "Then we've only got to climb the stairs and we'll be inside the highest flowerpot tower. Come on!"

The Sideways Crack was halfway up the wall of Dame Taffeta's quarters, which stood above Dame Honey's.

They pushed the banner through, and wriggled after it. Through the disgusting smell of the bellflowers, Dame Taffeta's room still smelled faintly of lavender. They passed through and ran up the steps which wound up through the dark hole in the flowerpot roof. This was the highest flowerpot tower. As usual, it was empty and still.

"It's very dark in here," Sesame said.

"Ow!" said Tiptoe, falling over Sprout with a thump.

"It's just the plant, blocking out the light," Brilliance said. She stared up at the hole in the flowerpot ceiling, where they usually wriggled through to the roof. It was completely covered by the plant. Then she tugged at the leaves covering the window. There was a gleam of daylight.

"Look at Flea!" Kelpie gasped. "He's huge!"

Flea was now the size of a rabbit. He

was fast asleep down in the courtyard.

"Anyone got a honeycake?" Brilliance said. "We have to get Flea up here. I've got a brilliant idea!"

No one had a honeycake. Kelpie found a yellow bellflower growing in the corner of the flowerpot. She pulled it off the plant and carried it to the window.

"Flea!" she called. "Yummy flower!"

Flea opened his eyes. His wings quivered at the sight of the flower.

"Tell us your plan, Brilliance," said Nettle.

"Naughty Fairies," Brilliance began.

"Not now," Nettle snapped. "This is an emergency!"

Brilliance pouted. "I'm going to tie the banner to Flea's feet," she said at last.

"Brilliant!" Sesame and Tiptoe exclaimed together.

"Told you," Brilliance said modestly.

"Flea's coming!" Kelpie said. "Get ready!"

Through the window, Brilliance hooked her finger around one of Flea's enormous toes. Flea kicked and buzzed crossly.

"The banner, quick!" Brilliance yelled at the other fairies. "I can't hold on for much longer!"

Tiptoe and Sesame quickly tied the end of the banner to Flea's toe.

"One, two, three . . . let go!" Brilliance shouted.

Flea rose above the flowerpots. The banner followed him like a long, multi-coloured tail.

"Fantastic!" Nettle squealed.

"Go, Flea, go!" Tiptoe and Sesame jumped up and down. Sprout squeaked.

"That's my bee," Kelpie said proudly.

Brilliance stared anxiously out of the window. Where was the imp? Where was the millipede? Was the banner facing the right way? And what if the

Humans at the House saw Flea before the imp did?

"We have to go back to the dormitory!" she told the others. "Quick, before the imp gets here!"

The Naughty Fairies rushed back through the Cracked Corridor and down to the Butterfly Stables. Every time they touched a yellow flower, there was a shower of stinking pollen. Even Kelpie looked a bit green by the time they reached their dormitory.

Dame Honey and Dame Taffeta were asleep on Brilliance and Nettle's beds. Their wands lay next to them, smoking gently.

"They must be tired," Tiptoe said. "Look, they've tried to burn the roots."

The roots of the plant were black and twisted, and clusters of yellow flowers lay trampled on the floor. Brilliance peered through the window, looking for the imp.

The Nettle Patch suddenly gave a shiver, and a large brown millipede raced into the St Juniper's courtyard. On the millipede's back sat the imp.

There was a muffled noise from deep inside the Butterfly Stables as the other fairies cheered. Brilliance and the others thumped each other on the backs with delight.

"Who's calling me a WIMP?" the imp screamed. He jumped down from the millipede and shook his fist at the banner.

"We are!" Brilliance yelled. She waved out of the window at the imp.

"You again!" the imp snarled. He flexed his thin blue fingers. "I'm coming up there to teach you a lesson!"

"Brilliant!" Brilliance said happily.

"I'm scared," Sesame said, as the imp jumped on to the plant and started climbing up to their dormitory window.

"There's nothing to be scared of," Kelpie said. "Unless he farts. Then we're in trouble."

"Ha!" said the imp, leaping through the window into the room.

"Ha yourself," said Brilliance. "Idiot."

The imp seemed to notice the plant for the first time.

"You fairy fool!" he said. "You planted those seeds, didn't you? And I suppose you want me to stop this plant from growing?"

One of the bellflowers sprinkled pollen on Brilliance's nose. She tried not to gag. "Why would I want to stop this fantastic plant from growing?" she said to the imp.

"You were supposed to crush the seeds, not plant them!" the imp shouted, stamping his foot.

"Like I care," Brilliance said. "So, how's Wiggle?"

The imp's expression changed. "Beautiful," he said fondly.

"I thought he was the stupidest millipede I'd ever seen," Brilliance said.

The imp's face turned ugly. "You like your little plant, hmm?" he said, narrowing his eyes at Brilliance.

Brilliance sniffed the nearest flower. "It's gorgeous," she squeaked.

"Mmm," Nettle added weakly.

"Ha!" the imp said again. "Time to say bye-bye!" A jet of black fire shot from his fingertip, straight at the plant. Flowers began to close. Leaves curled up and vanished.

"Yes!" Brilliance shouted. "I mean –
no! No!"

"Our beautiful plant!" said Nettle,
and coughed.

"Boo hoo," Tiptoe added.

Kelpie looked sad.

"Hee hee!" the imp said gleefully.
"This plant will vanish back into the
seeds by dusk, and they will never
grow again!"

"Will they still make perfect fairy
dust?" Sesame asked. "You . . . pooey . . .

parp." She wasn't very good at insults.

"Of course," the imp sneered.

"The plant will return to seed by dusk?" Brilliance repeated.

"Yes, yes!" the imp giggled. "Enjoy it while you can!"

"And I suppose you're going to make my bumblebee small again?" Kelpie said, glaring hard at the imp. "You stinking piece of pond scum!"

"Kelpie sounds just like normal," Tiptoe whispered to Sesame.

"Your wish is my command," said the imp with a nasty smile.

He pointed at Flea, who was still swooping around the courtyard, and muttered something. Then he somersaulted out of the window and landed on the millipede's back. The millipede snorted and reared, before galloping back into the Nettle Patch.

The fairies cheered.

"We did it!" Nettle said.

"Told you my plan was brilliant," Brilliance said.

Sesame and Tiptoe danced around Sprout as a normal-sized Flea buzzed joyfully into the dormitory.

"Where's your banner, Flea?" Kelpie asked, tickling him under the chin.

"Out in the courtyard," said Sesame happily. "Too big to stay on his normal-sized toe, I guess."

"Do you think we'll have lessons this afternoon?" Tiptoe asked.

They walked down the corridor and pushed through the thinning plant hanging over the courtyard door.

"I expect so," Nettle said gloomily.

In the courtyard, the bluebells started ringing.

"See?" Nettle said. "It's Science now."

"Maybe Dame Taffeta won't wake up in time to give us the fairy dust test," Tiptoe said hopefully.

Brilliance gasped. "The test!" she

cried. "The plant won't turn back into seeds until dusk, and the test is this afternoon! What are we going to do?"

"There's still Plan B," Kelpie said.

"Twinkle-tastic," said Sesame. Her eyes gleamed. "Crawly time!"

7

Super Sensitive Spider Silk

The Naughty Fairies ran round the back of the Science Flowerpot. The beetle, the wasp, the cricket and the three remaining ants were all resting quietly in the shade.

"Everyone will come into the classroom in a minute!" Tiptoe hissed, peering over the window sill. "We have to hurry up!"

Nettle put her ear spiders on a blade of grass, where they started spinning. The fairies tied the silk into loops and knots around the crawlies, being extra careful to keep the ants and the beetle apart. Sesame slipped the last knot over the beetle's head. She passed the end to

Brilliance, who threaded it through the
window.

"This spider silk is super sensitive,"
she told the others. "Even if I pull it
really gently, all the crawlies will come
through the window. So you've all got
to be ready for it. OK?"

Dame Lacewing was standing by the door as Brilliance, Nettle, Kelpie, Tiptoe and Sesame raced into the classroom. She was holding the register. "No running or flying inside the flowerpots," she said.

The Naughty Fairies skidded to a halt. Brilliance tried to breathe normally. She could see the spider silk hanging through the flowerpot window. A brown-haired fairy called Marigold was about to sit down at the window desk. Brilliance itched to run over and push her off the acorn chair.

"Congratulations, by the way," said Dame Lacewing. She sounded quite impressed.

"Thank you, Dame Lacewing," Brilliance said. "The imp said the plant would return to the seeds by dusk. It won't grow again."

"You have saved the school," Dame Lacewing said.

"Do we get a reward?" Kelpie asked.

"Yes," Dame Lacewing said. "No detention for planting the seeds in the first place."

"It was a bird," Brilliance began.

Dame Lacewing raised her hand for silence. "To your seats," she said. "Dame Taffeta is setting the class a fairy dust test today."

"Where is Dame Taffeta, Dame Lacewing?" one of the other fairies called from the back of the flowerpot.

"Still asleep on Brilliance's bed," Tiptoe whispered to Sesame.

"Dame Taffeta will be along shortly," Dame Lacewing said.

There was still a smudge of smelly pollen on Brilliance's arm. She stood next to the window desk and fiddled with a pot of sowbane that was sitting on the windowsill.

"Pooh," said Marigold. "Where's that smell coming from?"

"There's a bunch of those yellow flowers outside the window," Brilliance said, "The imp said they smell stronger as they die."

"Do you want to sit here, Brilliance?" Marigold offered.

"What's it worth?" Brilliance asked. She leaned a little closer.

Marigold coughed. "You can have my carrot cake tonight," she said.

"OK," said Brilliance. She settled down at the window desk and reached for the end of the spider silk. She could hear the wasp buzzing outside.

"As soon as Dame Lacewing gives out the test papers, I'll pull the silk," Brilliance whispered to Nettle, who was sitting behind her. "Pass it on."

A bright green and pink beetle trotted through the flowerpot door. It had a petal stuck to its back.

Dame Taffeta leaned down and picked up the petal. "Thank you, Pipsqueak,"

she said to the beetle. She read the
petal. Then she looked up at the class.
"I have an announcement," she said.

Brilliance tightened her grip on the
spider silk.

"Dame Taffeta has been taken ill,"

Dame Lacewing said. "She has suffered a reaction to the yellow flowers, and she won't be in this afternoon. She will give you your fairy dust test tomorrow."

"Yes!" Brilliance shouted, and jumped to her feet.

The beetle zoomed through the window. It was closely followed by the wasp, and then the cricket, and then the ants. Flea followed, buzzing happily. All the fairies started yelling.

"Oops," Brilliance said, staring at the silk in her hand.

It took the rest of the Fairy Science lesson to catch the crawlies.

"It's just as well that the spider silk broke," Nettle said, as they walked up to their dormitory after dinner. The sun was beginning to set and darkness was creeping across St Juniper's. "No one traced the crawlies to you, Brilliance."

"Dame Lacewing was looking at you

very strangely though," Sesame said, stroking Sprout.

"She was probably just wondering how I got the imp to shrink the plant," Brilliance said with a shrug. "I might tell her some day."

Tiptoe opened her bedside drawer and pulled out a box of sugared buttercups to celebrate. Kelpie gave hers to Flea.

Brilliance looked thoughtfully at the plant on the windowsill. There was just one flower left. She put her finger inside the flower and took a dab of pollen. Then she put her finger in her mouth.

"Ugh!" Nettle, wrinkled her nose.

"Yum," Kelpie said, watching Brilliance. Flea looked a bit dreamy.

Brilliance screwed up her face and swallowed. "There!" she said.

"What did you do that for?" Sesame asked in alarm.

Brilliance gave a brilliant smile.

"I always wanted to be taller," she said.